Soft Rock

ALSO BY DAN DEWEESE

You Don't Love This Man
Disorder
Gielgud

Soft Rock

•

DAN DEWEESE

A PROPELLER LONGFORM ORIGINAL

Copyright © 2023 by Dan DeWeese

All rights reserved. Except for brief passages quoted in critical articles or reviews, no part of this book may be reproduced in any form or by any means, electronic or mechanical, including photocopying and recording, or by any information storage and retrieval system, without permission in writing from the Publisher.

First U.S. edition, 2023
Cover design by No Hipness / Donald Geary
Cover figure from *Self-Portrait* by Henri Fantin-Latour, 1859
Interior design by Rachel Sensate

10 9 8 7 6 5 4 3 2 1

Published by Propeller Books, Portland, Oregon.
ISBN 978-1-955593-07-6

www.propellerbooks.com

SOFT ROCK

I

When I was five my father divorced my mother and moved to Los Angeles to write movies. I rooted for him but as the years passed every movie that opened in our local two-screen theater had one quality in common: it was not written by my father. I confirmed this by studying the small type on the "Now Playing" posters that hung in the theater's front windows. The posters taught me that movies are written by many people. They can be written by *Name & Name* or by *Name & Name and Name* or even by *Name & Name and Name & Name.* There are further variations but my father's name didn't appear in any of them and I stopped expecting Hollywood news from him.

My mother passed away a number of years ago. On my phone I keep a photo of her from when she was young: long hair pulled back, brown eyes in a heart-shaped face, thin Dutch lips. My mother's parents were natives of the small town in Idaho where I grew up. They ran a pawnshop on the short stretch of fading businesses people called *downtown* and they held a dim view of people, probably because they were often dealing with them in moments of desperation. My grandfather had back problems that made it difficult for him to sit for extended periods so he stood behind the counter of the pawnshop while my grandmother bustled around, moving one item here, another there, straightening and fixing things. At the end of the day they went home to dinner, which my grandfather ate standing at the kitchen counter while discussing items people had brought into the shop. My grandparents had multiple Bibles in their home, maybe one to a room, and were not shy about consulting them. They also had Precious Moments figurines, collectible plates with images of U.S. Presidents or Elvis Presley, and in a sideboard an entire collection of china my grandmother had pulled from the pawnshop. My grandmother often referred to the china—*Should we use the china?* she would ask, *Maybe we should use the china?*—but my grandfather dismissed it. I cannot recall an occasion on which he agreed they should use the china. My grandmother's ownership of the china and my grandfather's refusal to use it was probably an unspoken compromise.

This was not the only unspoken understanding in their house. In fact, years passed before I was able to connect conversational patterns there to events that preceded my existence—namely, the disappearance of my mother's siblings. My mother had two older brothers, John and Mark. John, the oldest, was drafted and went to Vietnam in the belief that it was his duty to defend the American way against Communism. He was killed in action within six months. My mother told me she was staying the night at a friend's house the evening her parents were informed of John's death. When her friend's parents dropped her back at home the next day, she said, everything had changed. *Everything changed after John died* is a sentence my mother repeated in various formulations throughout my childhood. Her brother Mark was not drafted but made sure, upon graduating from high school a year after his brother's death, to burn his draft card. He also grew his hair and "smoked dope." After a heated argument with his father a few weeks after graduation he took money from the pawnshop cash register, bought a bus ticket to San Francisco, and disappeared. The only contact he maintained with the family was through letters he wrote my mother. Over the years he mailed maybe a dozen of these letters and my mother filed them in a shoebox. One day when

I was in middle school I snuck into my mother's room and pulled this shoebox from her closet shelf and read the letters. Most didn't have return addresses and the few that did didn't feature the same address more than once. My mother's name was Alexandra but Mark's salutations were goofs: *Dear Allie*, or *Hey Lexi*, or *Miss Axela Andress*, or *Alexandra Salamandra*. Mark wrote of my mother's need to "get out from under the thumb" of their parents, of their life in small town Idaho as "a prison" from which he had escaped and from which she, too, must escape, of the different kinds of "mind expansion" he had experienced through LSD, and of the ways in which this mind expansion revealed the "fraudulence of religion," the "oppressions of the establishment," and the "pathology of the nuclear family." I found Mark's first few letters interesting and the rest repetitions. I don't know how many of the letters my mother shared with her parents. She may even have plucked them from the mailbox before her parents saw them at all. She told me she answered the letters that had return addresses. She also said she mailed Mark an invitation to her high school graduation and that during the ceremony, when she was sitting on a folding chair on the high school football field with the two hundred other members of her graduating class, she looked up and saw Mark sitting in the highest corner of the stands. He was wearing sunglasses and a baseball hat and was well away from where her parents sat in the clustered middle. She waved, she said, and the man in sunglasses and the baseball hat waved back, but when the ceremony ended and the students threw their mortar boards in the air and families and friends and teachers and strangers flooded the field the man in sunglasses and the baseball hat was not among them. *And I never saw him again*, my mother told me. *But I know it was him. I know he was there.*

Families rejected by one of their children carry a particular burden, and though this burden fell most heavily on my grandparents, I think my mother, too, was pained by it. This, at least, is how I explain her decision not to attend college. She didn't even apply. After graduating high school she kept her same room in her same home. She took a job at a printing company for no reason other than that they put a help wanted ad for an entry-level secretary in the newspaper. Alexandra became that secretary and it was at that printing company that she met Randall Marteau, who worked in sales. The printing company printed the phonebooks for all of the small towns in that part of Idaho. Randall's job was to find clients other than the phonebook publishers. The company owned a Toyota Celica that Randall drove from town to town to meet with prospective clients. I suspect this modest travel, combined with his bright-eyed friendliness, may have lent him a veneer of sophistication. He and Alexandra were a couple within six weeks of her hiring, and a few months later she was pregnant. When she told Randall, he invited her to a trade show he was attending in Reno. After the show's morning meet-and-greet, Randall and Alexandra drove to a chapel, were married, and returned in time for Randall to attend the trade show's afternoon sessions. When my mother told her parents about her pregnancy and Reno they were outraged. They had already lost both of their sons, though, so they decided to keep Alexandra close by offering her and Randall a stake in the pawnshop. My father told me leaving the printing company and accepting the pawnshop offer was the critical mistake. *Everything followed from the pawnshop offer*, he said. *You don't own the pawnshop, the pawnshop owns you.* My mother and her parents were always taking things from the pawnshop, he said. He would come home from working in the pawnshop and find, in his home, things from the pawnshop. *But it's beautiful*, he said my mother would say as she defended a collection of Fiestaware or a royal blue ottoman or a rocking chair with birds carved in the arms. Randall said he walked into the pawnshop once and ran into my mother on her way out, a stuffed and mounted mallard duck in her arms. *But it's beautiful*, she said. Their television set, which did not work properly, was from the pawnshop. Their drinking glasses with faded images of Denver Broncos wide receivers were from the pawnshop. Randall said he told my mother they were people who had jobs, they should buy things new, from stores, the way normal people did, but my mother continued to bring things home from the pawnshop. It was practically stealing if you thought about it, Randall told me. If you looked at the contracts and the agreements and the way the business was supposed to be run, it was virtually theft. He was supposed to share in the profits from the business, he said, but how were there ever going to be profits from the business when so much of the inventory was going out the door in the hands of the very people who owned the business? *Every dream I had was dying*, he told me. *Every dream I had was being murdered by the pawnshop.* So one day he, like Mark, took money from the cash register—he maintained and was adamant this money was owed him— and took a van to the Boise airport and bought a one-way ticket to Los Angeles. He called my mother from a payphone at the airport in Los Angeles and told her he would not be home that evening because he no longer lived in Idaho. There was not another woman, he said. What there was was the pawnshop and his desire to have nothing to do with it. I find this story amazing. My father has never, to my knowledge, made another decision even remotely this dramatic.

It's likely I was never told the entirety of the circumstances, but things didn't go well between my mother and her parents after that. My mother didn't want to work in the pawnshop any more than my father did. Working in the pawnshop may have been convenient when I was small and needed watching but the degree to which little was being asked of Alexandra beyond arranging large items—mostly televisions and musical instruments—on shelves, and arranging smaller items—mostly jewelry and knives—in glass cases made the job repetitive and boring. Randall had left to pursue his dreams and my mother wanted the same. She began to go on what she called "weekend trips." These trips were sometimes taken with friends and other times with boyfriends. I had no problem with this. When my mother was out of town I stayed with my grandparents, who left me alone. They never asked me about school and often cited situations in which they felt someone was "overthinking things." My mother was often one of these people "overthinking things." She began to go on trips more often, occasionally for more than just a weekend, and more of my clothing, toys, and belongings migrated to my grandparents' house. Though I now realize my mother was a young woman who may have told herself she would pursue her dreams after her child was grown but then found it impossible to wait, at the time I was not overthinking things. I was a boy who played with other children in the neighborhood and I ate my dinner and I did my schoolwork. If my mother was gone more than other children's mothers, how was I to know? I didn't keep track of other children's mothers. Sometimes I was with my mother, sometimes I was with my grandparents. Adults went on trips. Children visited grandparents. That was life. I did not care how many parents or grandparents watched other children. I did not care who lived where and who worked and at what. The census is taken once a decade and not by children. I cared whether a friend had toys or a dog, whether the friend was nice or the dog was mean. It was fun to play games, less fun to be punched. When I ran through a friend's living room or back yard, sometimes a father would be present. This father might frown and tell us to slow down but that was the extent of the moment. These were isolationist fathers. They had their garages and their basements and their sports and their boats. They established their territories and protected them and did not otherwise intervene. They did not know my father and my father did not know them. Fathers kept to their business and their business was building boards at the plant or fixing cars at the shop or selling chairs at the store. And it's not as if I was estranged from my own father. When I was twelve, in fact, I spent an entire July with my father and his girlfriend. I slept on the futon in the living room of their apartment in Santa Monica. Waking up in Santa Monica was like waking up on one of the planets in the science-fiction stories I liked to read. There were humanoid lifeforms but they were aliens, and there was a reality but it was alternate. Randall had returned to his original vocation: he worked in sales at a printing company. Elise, his girlfriend, worked for a company that handled music publicity. I'm not sure what her job was but there were stacks of promotional compact discs sitting next to the living room stereo bearing the names of bands I'd never heard of. On weekdays Randall and Elise went to work and then came home and ate dinner and watched television. On weekends Randall tinkered with his screenplays. This all struck me as sophisticated. When Randall and Elise left for work in the morning Randall gave me five dollars and a key to the apartment. I would watch television for a bit and then walk to the outdoor mall. One day I accidentally left the key on the kitchen counter and locked myself out of the apartment. It was sunny and warm and I had my five dollars so I acted casual and headed to the mall. On the way I passed an abandoned box on the sidewalk filled with old paperbacks. A book about a man's experience being abducted by aliens was on top and I took it and walked to the mall and sat on a bench in the shade. At noon I bought a ham sandwich and a bag of chips for five dollars. I drank water from a fountain near the bathrooms. The day seemed long but the book about the aliens was interesting. If you don't want to be abducted by aliens, live in a city. They grab rural home dwellers and men camping solo and they do it at night and you wake up the next morning naked in your yard or the forest, piecing together fragments of memory. While I sat on the bench reading, a man in dark blue jeans and a crisp white short-sleeve dress shirt sat down next to me and sighed. After a few minutes he asked how my book was. I had been taught not to give information to strangers so I shrugged and said it was okay. He said my mom was lucky I was happy to read a book by myself while she shopped. I said pretty much. He kept looking around and then sighed again. To my mind this behavior qualified him as a pervert so I stood and went into a bookstore and browsed within view of the front desk. At five o'clock I left the store and walked home looking over my shoulder every so often. The pervert was nowhere to be seen and I was sitting on the building's front steps when Randall and Elise came home. Randall said he understood I might enjoy reading in the sun but it was probably best if I didn't sit in front of the building like that because not everyone passing by was normal or trustworthy. The mall was fine, he said, there were plenty of people at the mall, but a kid sitting alone on the street was different. I said okay and I followed him and Elise up the steps to the apartment and when he unlocked the door I walked in and grabbed my key from the kitchen counter. They didn't realize I'd been locked out and I felt I'd pulled an amazing caper. Who knew what I might be capable of next? Randall talked to me about writing screenplays, how the hero had to have a goal and the goal had to be clear within the first thirty pages. Every page is a minute, he said, watch a clock when you watch movies and you'll see the hero has his goal in thirty minutes. He said the hero had to go after the goal with total focus and suffer a death moment but not really die. *Screenplays are structure*, he said more than once. *Screenplays are clockwork*. There are other steps the hero has to go through but I've forgotten them. Eventually the hero wins. Randall owned a number of different books about how to write screenplays but they all agreed about the hero. He owned a VCR and we watched *Star Wars* on it a number of times and he talked about the structure. When my California month was over I didn't want to go home to Idaho, I wanted to stay in Santa Monica forever. When I returned to Idaho I said as much to my mother. I understood my father had left us and it wasn't fair to me and it wasn't fair to my mother but he lived where things happened and he talked about interesting puzzles, the puzzle of what made a thing a movie, the puzzle of how to get a screenplay into the right hands, the puzzle of how to make it in the industry. It was heartless of me to say these things but it was how I felt. My mother never sent me to California again. I am not saying it was because of what I said, I am just reporting a sequence of events. There was a summer where my grandparents took me on a road trip to Colorado to see the Continental Divide, there was a summer where I mowed lawns for the landscaping company of a man who was probably dating or trying to date my mother, and there were summers where I was busy with other things. I spent significant time during these summers riding my bike around town and having a fine time, buying sodas and candy bars at the convenience store and occasionally shoplifting a *Playboy* or a *Penthouse*. In college I was briefly smitten with a girl in my group of friends and in a moment of playfulness in the dining hall she said she could guess what my father was like, that he must have been a disciplined person who gave me lists of chores to do and taught me manners. *I bet he didn't let you get away with anything,* she said. *I can tell from the way you carry yourself.* Everyone laughed. I smiled and said nothing. My father wrote me letters and later emails but there was nothing in them about chores or manners. He wrote about movies he'd seen, the ones he felt were good and the ones he felt were not. He mentioned his admiration for a Richard Dreyfuss movie called *Moon Over Parador* more than once. He couldn't stand *Goodfellas* or any Martin Scorsese movies. He said they were nasty and exploitative and Scorsese would eventually be unmasked. He married Elise, they had a boy and a girl, and they moved to Rancho Cucamonga. He still works in sales for the same printing company. He has never sold a screenplay. I don't think he tried very hard. Even if he hasn't been much involved in my life he has never lied to me and I respect this. He has done well for himself, is a good person, and we are on good terms.

Every Christmas he sends me a card with a check for fifty dollars in it.

II

The years in which my father and Elise were raising my half-brother and half-sister in Rancho Cucamonga, I was busy finishing high school and after that occupied with my studies at The Evergreen State College in Olympia, Washington. Evergreen is the kind of college in which you either flunk out or do fine, and I did fine. I majored in Humanities and wrote a thesis on the aesthetics of NFL Films in comparison to the literature and philosophy of Heian-era Japan. In the longest chapter I used *The Pillow Book* as an ur-text that informed and anticipated American media coverage of the 1967 Ice Bowl, in which the Green Bay Packers defeated the Dallas Cowboys for the NFL Championship. My time at Evergreen passed like a dream. Just before I graduated, though, my grandparents decided to sell the pawnshop and retire, but there was some kind of legal entanglement regarding the part ownership they had offered my father when he was married to my mother. There remained a document on file that suggested my father owned a percentage of the pawnshop, and my grandparents couldn't sell the pawnshop without a commitment to pay all interested parties. They looked into challenging the document but a lawyer explained that his fee would negate any proceeds from a victory so my grandparents sold the shop and mailed Randall an envelope that included a terse statement and a check. Randall didn't want the money. He told me it would be "bad hoodoo" for him to take it and it would be better for the money to go to me. He either did not see or did not realize this was the wrong time for me to be given a large sum of money. I graduated from Evergreen, moved to Portland, Oregon, rented an apartment in the southeast quadrant, bought a used car, new furniture, a big television, and a surround-sound audio system. Even after these expenditures there was money left, which meant I didn't have to look for work, so I didn't. Instead, I drifted. I wanted to turn my collision of NFL Films and Heian-era Japan into a book but this would require work for which there was no longer a deadline. I watched television and YouTube videos during the day and spent my evenings watching movies and smoking weed. As my few college friends fell out of touch I stayed in my apartment for longer and longer periods of time, drifting further. I convinced myself my television and YouTube viewing were research for my book. A prodigious number of old NFL games could be found on YouTube in its early months. People had football games recorded on old VHS tapes and they transferred them to their computers and so here came the Sunday afternoon and Monday night matchups from the nineteen eighties. The graphics, the announcers' introductions, the camera angles and slow-motion instant replays, they fascinated me. They fascinate me still. And though there is of course no right time to lose a parent, this was a particularly bad time to lose my mother. She told me on the phone that she had been diagnosed with ovarian cancer but that they had caught it in time—she felt fine and would beat it. I couldn't tell if this was true or just the response of a woman who hadn't achieved her dreams and believed the world owed her more time to pursue them. I won't pretend to know what my mother's dreams were. I suspect they were dreams of abstractions, like freedom and love. She had various boyfriends over the years but the relationships always dissolved after a year or two. She didn't seem interested in marrying again and the breakups didn't seem to faze her. What was more important than anything else, she would say, was to maintain a *positive mental attitude*.

I have only recently begun to consider the ways in which children may be unable to see their parents with any degree of accuracy. For instance, I believed my mother repeated her admonitions about the value of a *positive mental attitude* as a form of parenting. It now seems odd to me that she felt the need to bring this up so often. I assumed these were parenting moments but now wonder if they were parenting moments at all. Was she parenting me or parenting herself? Similarly, I believed I was a partner in the conversations we had during my childhood. I assumed my mother was speaking to me but now wonder if she was speaking to me at all. Was she in conversation with me or in conversation with herself? She had favorite topics and circled back to them. She often brought up her brother Mark. She didn't understand why he hadn't contacted her, and she wanted to find him. I assumed he was dead. My understanding was that AIDS killed a frightening percentage of gay men in San Francisco in those years, many of them estranged from their families. A fair number probably lived under different names or were purposely unfindable. I'm not saying I knew Mark was gay. I never met him, I have no idea. It's a private theory I've never said aloud. I suppose it's just the way I explain a young man disappearing in San Francisco, never to return. When my mother called again and said she was adjusting to the fact she was indeed ill, she assured me it wasn't dire. She sounded tired but I believed her. We should go to the lake soon, she said. If she paid for it, would I come out to the lake, maybe for a week? She seemed uncertain, as if worried the request was an imposition. I said are you talking about next summer? You're not talking about going to the lake now, right? She said yes, of course, she meant next summer. I said I would probably be done with my book on the Ice Bowl and Heian-era Japan by the summer and would be ready for a break—the lake sounded good. I'm glad you're still pursuing your interest in sports, she said. I reminded her I wasn't pursuing an interest in sports, I was pursuing an interest in collision studies. Sports were a subcategory of culture and culture could best be understood through the carefully managed collisions of cultural objects or processes. That was my work. She said okay, well, she was glad I was still pursuing my interest in collisions. We could talk more about the Ice Bowl or about Japan soon. I said that sounded good.

Two weeks later my father called to tell me my mother was dead. I didn't understand why my grandparents hadn't warned me. Had my mother hidden her illness from them? Had she hidden it from herself? If she hadn't hidden her illness from my grandparents, had they hidden it from me? I dropped the phone and tore my apartment apart, throwing things against the walls, breaking plates and glasses. A neighbor knocked on the door and I opened it and told him my mother was dead and if he didn't leave me alone he would also be dead and I slammed the door and resumed destruction. When I called my father back he said he had just heard the news himself and was as confused as I was. He hadn't known my mother was sick at all. "But this has happened," he said. "We do not have to accept the way it happened, but we have to accept that it has happened." He told me my grandparents called him first because they blamed him and wanted him to know they blamed him. They weren't right in the head anymore, he said. They thought in conspiracies and vendettas and believed that because he had given me the money from the pawnshop I was somehow on his side and therefore against them. "Your mother loved you so much, and they love you, too, even if what they believe about their lives is a fantasy," he said. "Call them. It doesn't matter what they think about me."

So I called them. And then I drove to Idaho for the funeral. The pawnshop was owned by someone else now, and though my grandparents talked and talked, what they said didn't come to any point. They were physically healthy and took care of themselves but in conversation they repeated the same stories, talking in circles. My grandfather told me an anecdote about a transaction he recalled from the pawnshop, and in the middle of the anecdote he stopped to give me some background information he felt I needed in order to understand the anecdote. The background information turned out to be the very anecdote he was in the middle of telling, but he related the entire thing in earnest, unaware.

There was nothing more to be done, so I returned to Portland. My belief in my NFL Films and Heian-era Japan book wavered radically. When I woke up and had a cup of coffee my book seemed important and insightful and the kind of thing for which there was indeed a reading public. I would open the manuscript and read my Sei Shonagon criticism and then go onto YouTube and watch old NFL games. I kept scrupulous notes on the imagery and attitudes. After a few hours, though, when I had done little other than rearrange the sentences I had already written, maybe adding a hesitant thought about Shonagon (i.e. *Implication of others' inferior aesthetics primarily through tone. Shonagon's tone or translator's?*) and a hesitant thought about the NFL broadcasts (i.e. *Limited playbooks equals little to analyze equals commentary of aesthetics rather than technique? See Shonagon*) I would in certain moments realize what I was doing was highly unusual and perhaps did not have an audience after all. In the first hour of the day I could not only see the book in my mind but could feel it like a ghost or spirit energy in the room. I was summoning its presence and would call it into being. Later, though, this feeling would disappear. I could neither see nor feel the book and became painfully aware of the artificiality of everything I was doing and the degree to which it was a delusion. Every movement became mechanical. I was afflicted with a kind of psychological rheumatism. I would decide that what I believed was a book was maybe a documentary film but then think the documentary film was as much a delusion as the book. I would think maybe the book was really a magazine article and then feel the magazine article, too, was a delusion. I would tell myself the project was not a documentary or an article, that it wasn't useful to think of it as a documentary or an article, that it was either a book or not a book. I would powerfully feel it a book and then just as powerfully feel it a delusion. My mother was dead, my grandparents were garrulous, my father was in Rancho Cucamonga. I would tell myself to focus. What I needed to do each day was focus on completing whatever small piece I was working on that day. Focus on Sei Shonagon. Focus on NFL YouTube. Focus on my notes, focus on my writing. All of this of course sounds strange and sad but at least I wasn't selling sham mortgages or writing radio ads. I was just trying to think. And also of course smoking a lot of weed. At a certain point I replaced my morning cup of coffee with weed. This was maybe a mistake but when stoned everything seemed possible. My book seemed not only real but as good and as necessary as any book. It had the quality, at least, of being original.

In my mind's eye I saw glossy photo spreads in the book: photos of footballs spinning through gray winter skies above receivers' outstretched arms, paintings of Japanese women brushing their long black hair, a photo of Jack Buck calling a game, a painting of Sei Shonagon raising an eyebrow. At a certain point I stopped writing. I just smoked weed and read old books and watched old football games. All sorts of people smoked and read and watched, so there was no longer anything singular about what I was doing and it occurred to me I was in trouble. Yes I could simply have gotten a job, but I didn't need one. Yes I could simply have finished the book, but the world wasn't asking for it. There is a phrase I have heard: *youthful folly*. Maybe I was engaged in *youthful folly*. Who hasn't been? What was definitely happening was I was drifting. I needed a way forward. A few of my friends from Evergreen had gone to graduate school and I thought maybe that was a good step, maybe it could save me. I addressed a single email to everyone I could think of and Oscar, an old classmate from Evergreen, responded. He had also moved to Portland, he said, and was currently in a graduate program at the city college downtown. Graduate school was easy, he said. He was having the time of his life. There was a particular professor in the Department of English by the name of Kellogg and if I went in and talked to Professor Kellogg, Oscar said, I would see I had options.

I looked up Professor Kellogg's office hours and visited him that same week. His third-floor office featured a faded yellow steel desk and a tall set of bookshelves that, in addition to books, held empty tissue boxes, dented canteens, a limp spider plant, and considerable dust. A slim, dirty window offered a view of multiple floors of similarly slim, dirty windows surrounding a dark and muddy courtyard. Kellogg had white hair, a white beard, and white dandruff on the shoulders of his moss-colored sweater. He moved a stack of books from the vinyl cushion of a metal chair so I could sit. The impression the books left in the vinyl suggested it had been some time since Kellogg had hosted anyone. A green banner on the wall read "Go Viks!" and I was mystified for a long moment before I realized the school mascot was the Vikings. The spelling on the banner suggested the existence of a person or creature called a "Vik," however, and I wondered not only how a university could so brazenly flaunt an inability to spell but also why a professor would further the error by hanging it on his wall. Was Kellogg still actively teaching? Was he retired but with access to this ceremonial office in which he might sit? After he placed his books on the floor and settled into his chair he asked what he could do for me. I told him I was considering graduate studies and a friend had recommended I discuss it with him. He seemed surprised by this. Discuss what with him, he asked. I didn't know what to say other than to repeat that the issue was my speculative graduate studies. He looked at me as if trying to tell whether I was lying. Because I was not lying I had no defense for his look and began instead to tell him things about myself. He was struck by the fact that I had attended Evergreen. It seemed to signify something to him, whether positive or negative I couldn't tell. He asked about my classes there and I handed him the syllabus of Collision Studies, the course in which I had initiated my work on Sei Shonagon and the Ice Bowl. He looked it over for a moment. "Is there a book list or a schedule?" he said. "This syllabus looks like an essay. It's entirely in prose." I explained the course was writing intensive and that everyone was encouraged to write through their thoughts, the professor included. Kellogg began to read the syllabus aloud: "It has long been established in the humanities that everything is, in its way, a text. This suggests that texts can be read through, over, against, or in support of each other. A film, for instance, can be read against a novel or play, just as a newspaper editorial can be read through a dance, or an art installation as commentary on the architecture of a public bathhouse. At the same time, something like a film retains its unique and intrinsic filmic qualities, just as pieces of literature retain their intrinsic literary qualities, by which I mean that a text like a film has, at its core, simultaneous textual and extra-textual energies. It is best not to think of these as apples-versus-oranges qualities, by which I mean comparative, not botanical, so much as perhaps astrophysical qualities, in which something like a collapsing star is both a part of our universe and, at its core, a phenomenon evolving toward, or falling into, if you prefer, a black hole that connects to something extra-universal or perhaps multiversal, i.e. *not* a part of our universe. In this course we will explore these energies, and I will ask you to produce a final text that serves as commentary on both the course-as-text, and on the text that is the syllabus you hold in your hands at this moment. All contributions are welcome, all modes of expression are valid, humanity is a protean concept and I intend to accept and respond with respect and benevolence to whatever iteration of humanity you are currently inhabiting or projecting." He placed the syllabus on the desk between us and gazed at it for a moment. I told him this course changed my life. He nodded. "Yes. This course changed your life." He said this as if he had been there. I told him the course was the genesis of my Heian-NFL collision studies. "Yes. I can see the course was the genesis of your Heian-NFL collision studies." He spoke with great seriousness but I could not tell what he meant. I am quick to detect sarcasm or irony but there was something unreadable in Kellogg, a mental screen behind which he was operating, and I could neither see through this screen nor cast it aside. He said he wasn't entirely sure he understood what I meant by "collision studies." This surprised me but I explained the basic principles: it was an aggressively generalist scholarship meant to counter the increasing specialization that was a feature of late capitalism, in which the marketplace offered increasingly specialized products, increasingly specialized cultural or pseudo-cultural experiences, and increasingly specialized forms of education entirely instrumentalized as training for a jobs market formed and controlled by the forces of late capitalism and relying upon a continued cult of the individual in which all members of society were encouraged to believe the fiction that they, too, were increasingly specialized in their desires, a kind of *ex post facto* logic that validated the existence of all the increasingly specialized products, culture, and degrees. Kellogg told me he wasn't sure he agreed with my reading of specialization. After all, he said, his own dissertation had not just been on modernism, and not just on the work of Joseph Conrad, but on particular shipwrecks in *Lord Jim* and the ways in which that novel's original readers would have understood its fictional shipwrecks to refer to actual, well-known shipwrecks, and how this meant the novel could, by those readers, have been read as a kind of nonfictional critique of maritime tragedy. I said but of course scholars of his generation had been made to produce incredibly specific dissertations in order to imply the existence of incredibly unique individuals who had produced the dissertations, and to then market these supposedly unique individuals as objects that might be purchased, fed, and watered by institutions. Kellogg told me the logical extension of my argument was not only that specialized knowledge did not exist, which was obviously incorrect, but that individuals themselves did not exist, which would invalidate any need for me, as an individual, to pursue an advanced degree. In fact, he said, since my theory was that the individual was a fiction, this suggested he and I did not actually exist, were not actually having the conversation we were having, and that it was therefore not only unnecessary for me to pursue a degree but in fact impossible. I told him this was outrageous, that it was an example of the exact sophistry holders of power use to validate their own perpetuation of the rigged capitalist market, that he was a fraud and his time was coming. If his own field was so real and valid, I said, why did he have a tiny office at the end of a forgotten hallway where he had clearly not been visited by anyone for months or, more likely, years? He turned to his bookshelf and with trembling hand began pulling down volumes. They were books he had written or contributed to: a book on Conrad, a book on transatlantic modernism, a book of essays on someone named Mina Loy. "Are these books not real?" he said. "Am I not now holding them?" His frenzy of ego was embarrassing and I left his office and the city college campus knowing it was not the place for me.

My argument with Professor Kellogg did not energize me, for no sooner had I left the building than I felt lost. It was cold and raining, people did not look at me, and the world did not care about me. I boarded a bus back across the river and exited two stops early to buy a cup of coffee and try to clear my head. In the coffeehouse, however, after I ordered and waited, they did not announce my drink. I stood in a conspicuous spot but the barista neither looked at nor spoke to me. Being ignored is the first step to becoming invisible and from there it is a dangerously slippery slope. The world wants us dead and history wants us forgotten. I know everyone feels this way—the need to fight drowning, even if it involves thrashing and shouting—but I felt it keenly that day. Eventually I asked the barista about my drink and she claimed to have no idea what I was talking about. I couldn't tell if she was being honest or covering but we had to start over and I stood there and stood there. All of this for an Americano. Finally she called out the drink. As I retrieved it I asked what blend they were using. I thought this a friendly-enough question but the barista seemed pained. "I can't keep track, we change all the time," she said. She asked the man at the register. He shrugged. I said they only had a few blends arranged for sale on the shelves—I would probably see right away which was the espresso. "What's out there isn't what we use back here," she said. This flummoxed me. The coffee they were serving in their drinks was different from the beans for sale? Yes, she said, the beans for sale were always the same but they used all sorts of things behind the bar. I said did she mean what they had behind the bar was higher-quality? "Maybe higher-quality, maybe lower-quality," she said. "Maybe some of one get mixed up with some of the other. I'm telling you I have no idea, I lost track long ago." She turned to make more drinks. It was clear our conversation was over and I left the coffeehouse.

I had no purpose and no prospects as I wandered past a block filled with a dozen or more three-story brick apartment buildings. Small trees, clipped lawns, and wide concrete paths separated the buildings. Their clean, square lines suggested they had been built in the nineteen-fifties. Artfully-placed vines climbed the sides of many of the buildings and as I looked up to admire a particular strand, I heard a song. The melody drifted from an open window on the third floor. I recognized the song but could neither name nor place it. It was a soft rock song that operated according to an obsolete aesthetic, a song I had heard on the radio as a child. Though it had not been a huge hit, it was clear to me the song was in many ways the apotheosis of the soft rock aesthetic. It suggested a mood and tone of adult life that many songs had suggested during my childhood but which I had never encountered beyond the songs themselves. The mood was one of elegant resignation, of melancholy expressed via languid sophistication. The song was not by anyone famous, no one had recorded anything like it since its release, and for a moment I was shattered. I know it is foolish to confuse songs with aspirations and that what is played on the radio is not documentary realism. It is also true, however, that music shows us the way. Though part of me is formed from the dirt of northern Idaho, another part of me is built on the foundation of *Led Zeppelin IV*. Everyone is this way. I was grateful to be hearing this perfect but forgotten song again not only because it was a perfect and forgotten part of culture, but because it, too, formed a part of me, and that part was also perfect and forgotten. I felt that whoever occupied that apartment would be a calm person of focus and discipline. It would be someone older than me, at peace with their place in society, quietly inspired and effortlessly effective. I was fuming over an argument with a dissipated professor at a university that could not spell the name of its own nonsensical mascot, but the person inhabiting the apartment was likely sipping tea while afloat on the melody of the song. As I stood there filled with these realizations, the song ended. No new song began. I heard the hiss of traffic from the nearby freeway and the caws of strutting crows. The person in the apartment did not need another song. They were enlightened and at work and when I recognized this I also recognized my own failure. I was wandering a maze of my own construction and could not get out. I felt shame and mortification and that the drivers on the freeway were fleeing me and the birds were jeering. I realized the song, its melody and tone, its pace and rhythm, was not just a beacon but also a path. "Hello?" I called toward the open window. "Is anybody there?" Mist filled the air. My eye chose a pinpoint bead and tracked it and lost it and chose another bead and tracked and lost that one, too. Infinite beads fell in infinite paths and my eye tried and failed again to track them. My shoulders ached beneath the weight of the books and folders in my backpack and I stood in the mist for some time, trying and failing to truly *see the mist*, before I realized the window was closed. I had neither seen nor heard it close. The complex was surrounded by a black iron fence with locked gates. No entry was possible.

I walked home tired but consoled. This much was clear: the song established a mood, it calmed and centered the listener, and calm centering was what I required. If I owned that song and could play it every day I would become the person I wanted to become. All that was necessary was to identify, find, and purchase the song.

III

I began the search the next day. I felt good, almost celebratory as I drove to the record store. If I did not yet own the song I had at least been reminded of its existence and knew it was out there. I would find it, buy it, play it, and ascend. But record store employees loathe a customer who asks for a song he cannot name by an artist he cannot name and I was hopeless as a singer, so I stepped into the nearest store knowing I had little choice but to flip through the entire compact disc section, artist by artist. In Jaycee's House of Music the process required nearly three hours. I was interrupted nine times by three different employees asking if I needed help and nine times I declined. I finished flipping through the W-Z section with a sense of shock: I had not found the song. I approached an employee and asked if there was a music store with a larger inventory than Jaycee's. We had a difficult exchange in which the employee tried to understand what I was looking for and I tried to explain that if I'd known what I was looking for I wouldn't have required help. "And yet you're looking for something specific, so you *do* know what you're looking for. It's just you can't name it," he said. I said even if I granted his point, would we be any nearer an answer? When he said he supposed not, I pointed out this meant his clarification was not meant to help me but merely to establish his own dominance. He seemed put off by this and said maybe I should try Music Millennium.

Music Millennium occupied an old brick building that descended the slope of East Burnside Street. Though the store had a larger inventory, my search of Jaycee's had sharpened my flipping skills and I was able to move through Music Millennium's compact discs in under two hours. The result, unfortunately, was the same: I did not come upon the band whose name I did not know, who had recorded the song whose title I did not know. I descended four steps each time I moved from one to another of the store's connected rooms but nothing among the used cd's jogged my memory, nor did any of the new or used DVD's. I skipped the jazz and classical sections and stepped down and through the narrow doorway into the last, lowest level. I was Dante in a musical inferno without a Virgil to guide me. What would I find in the vinyl room? The Kingston Trio half-melted and entombed in wax? A three-headed beast belching the hits of Pat Boone, Celine Dion, and Hanson? I spent two more hours flipping cardboard covers until my fingers were raw and my neck ached. I did not find the song. Instead I found the door, exited to the sidewalk, and watched traffic speed up the street while I considered how a merciful end to my search could be had by stepping in front of the next passing bus. I chose instead to cross the street and step into a restaurant deli to consider my options. I ordered from the deli counter and found a small table where I could take my roast beef sandwich and potato chips. What were the odds the song had been in one or both of the stores but I had overlooked it? It would involve two categories of error: either a manual error resulting in my somehow flipping past the album or a failure of vision in which I had seen the album but hadn't registered it. As the impossibility of calculating these odds with any degree of statistical accuracy began to dawn on me, I realized that not only was I humming the song while thinking all of this through but that I was humming the song because it was in fact *faintly audible at that very moment.* I was confused, I thought. My mind was playing tricks on me. But I listened closely and it was true: the song was playing through the restaurant's overhead speakers, barely detectable behind the clatter from the kitchen and the hum of conversation. People have phones now that can report the title of any song, but I doubt that would have helped even back then, since the restaurant's speakers were mounted at least fifteen feet overhead, at ceiling level. I flagged down an employee—whether she was a server or cook, I wasn't sure—and asked if she knew the name of the song playing. She listened for a moment and said, "Is it Fleetwood Mac?" I told her I knew Fleetwood Mac's catalogue inside out and it was not Fleetwood Mac. "I guess I don't know, then," she said.

"Would it be possible for you to find out?" I asked.

"Give me a minute," she said.

She took more than a minute. By the time she returned, the song had ended and another, lesser song was playing. She said she was sorry but the music was controlled through a computer in the manager's office and this office was locked while the manager was away on an errand. I asked if the manager would be back anytime soon. "Not until later tonight," she said.

I explained the situation: I had been searching for the song for years. So long, in fact, that I was willing to pay a fairly significant amount of money to anyone who entered the manager's office and checked the title and artist.

"Anyone who did that would be fired," the woman said. "I think it will just have to stay a mystery." She walked away without waiting to hear anything more from me. I assumed everyone else there also felt their job was more important than the title of a soft rock song.

So I had heard the song again and again it had eluded me. Had I failed in what would be my two best opportunities to discover the song, or was there some deeper reason this track, perfect and forgotten and unheard for years, had now unfurled twice for me? I did not take up further consideration of the question. I went home and spent the rest of the day smoking and watching the 1986 AFC championship game in which the Denver Broncos defeated the Cleveland Browns.

That choice might have been a search-ending response of pathetic laziness—or at least a serious procedural mistake—if not for what happened when I went to see Oscar a few days later to tell him how my meeting with Professor Kellogg had gone. Oscar also smoked but I caught him at a moment when he was unsupplied, so I told him my story while we went to see a friend of his. As we walked through multiple blocks I became so involved in narrating my outrage over the exchange with Kellogg that I paid scant attention to where we were going. Kellogg had played games with me, I said. How could Oscar have recommended I speak to the man when the man had been imperious and cold and condescending and deluded? Oscar did not seem particularly sorry or apologetic, responding instead with shrugs and expressions of surprise. When he stopped and said, "Here we are," I looked up and blinked: we were outside the same building from which I had first heard the song. Oscar pressed a button on the intercom next to the gate, it buzzed, and we entered.

The building's stairwell smelled of fresh paint, and people's wet shoes had left a damp path up the middle of the red-carpeted stairs. I hadn't said anything to Oscar about the song and felt a strong sense I should not. At the third floor I followed him down a hallway to an apartment whose door was ajar and we stepped into a small living room. Across the room was a window that looked out over the street. I became very calm—so calm, in fact, that I found myself stifling a yawn. A young man wearing a black sweatsuit sat in an old beige armchair, reading a magazine. His hair went every direction and his sweatsuit seemed a size too large. The high-zipped collar came to just beneath his chin and reminded me, for some reason, of Frankenstein. (I do not mean the monster.) I thought he might be on his way to exercise but a joint perched on an ashtray on the coffee table suggested a man at home for the time being. A detail far more important to me, however, was the presence of three large shelving units along one of the walls. The units rose nearly to the ceiling and were filled with records. In the room's far corner a chrome turntable sat atop a stereo cabinet that held an old or at least convincingly-retro receiver and amplifier. Somewhere in this room, I realized, was the sleeve that held the record that held the song. If I could find it I would become the man I was meant to be: productive, intellectual, possessed of insights into society and culture, able to lay bare the truths of our lives. Oscar introduced the man in the chair as his friend Dennis. Dennis nodded vaguely in my direction. I studied him carefully. This was the person who knew the song, who held it somewhere in his shelves. Oscar asked Dennis if he had any weed we could buy, but it was decided we would smoke first.

"I was walking by this building recently," I said to Dennis. "I think you were playing a song. I wonder if you remember."

"I play a lot of songs," he said.

"It was a soft rock song."

"I don't play soft rock."

"Maybe you think of it differently. I think of it as soft rock."

"Sorry. I don't know what to tell you. Not a soft-rock guy."

"Seventies music? Maybe one-hit wonders of the seventies?"

"I never sit down and say, You know, I think I'm gonna play some one-hit wonders of the seventies. That's not a thing."

"Maybe there's a compilation album you like."

"Maybe you're confused. Maybe you heard music from another apartment, or even another building. All these buildings are the same, you know."

I was getting nowhere so I changed tack. I asked about his record collection. What price could a person name that would make him sell the whole lot, I wondered. He said his records weren't for sale but I was welcome to look through them. Dennis and Oscar were musicians, so it wasn't long before they were making disparaging jokes about local bands. As I flipped through Dennis's records I felt the presence of the song, and a sense of wellbeing washed over me in a way that has happened only a handful of times in my life. A scent often accompanies the feeling. At a friend's house in grade school, it was an apple crumble his mother baked while we watched *Tron*. In my grandparents' home it was furniture polish. In a used record store in Olympia, Washington, it was not only the aged vinyl but also the cardboard covers and printed inserts. When this feeling occurs there is a homeowner or clerk or parent nearby who is busy, everything seems in its right place, and time slows in a way unrelated to the speed of light or the expansion of the universe or any of the other fantasies repeated by theoretical physicists. Dennis passed me a joint. I asked again if he didn't want to sell the lot. He said he'd spent years buying the records and as a musician and deejay, listening to them was part of his work. Besides, he said, there were a dozen record stores in town where I could buy my own copies for less than he would charge. I said but what I wanted was *his* collection. That made no sense, he said, a person should have a connection to the albums, you're supposed to start from scratch and discover new stuff and old stuff and odd stuff and overlooked stuff. I said well maybe I could buy hundreds of new and old and odd and overlooked albums and then he and I could switch collections. He said I was stoned and didn't know what I was saying. Could I at least listen to his records, I asked. He had started toward the kitchen but stopped. "Are you asking to borrow my records, or to sit and and listen to them here," he said.

"Whatever you're comfortable with," I said.

He looked at Oscar but I couldn't tell what passed between them. "Knock yourself out," he said. "Just be careful with everything. Oscar and I are going to take a walk."

"I don't think this is a good idea," Oscar said.

"You don't have to do anything," Dennis said.

"Whether or not I have to do anything isn't what I'm worried about."

"Then what are you worried about? Stop worrying when there's nothing to worry about."

They left without further explanation and I was alone with the records. I pushed Dennis's chair next to the window and put one on. I knew it wasn't the one on which I would find the song but it seemed smart to warm up the machine. I listened to the music and the sigh of distant traffic and the voices of passersby below and the shouts of children playing soccer on a field down the block. Together these sounds formed a single, peaceful symphony. The entirety of my life, it seemed, had been a journey to that apartment to put a record on at that moment and play my part. Were it practical I might have complimented the passersby on the tone of their conversation and cheered the kids for the quality of their chatter. I was not about to walk to the field, though, so I contented myself with the feeling of doing the right work in the right place. I removed the first record from the turntable, put a different one on, and wandered the apartment. Magazines lay strewn across the couch and kitchen counters and unopened mail filled a table near the door but the rooms were otherwise in order. I stepped into the bathroom intending only to use the toilet but realized it had been days since I'd bathed. I turned the shower on, undressed, and stepped in. The tub was stained pink around the drain and in streaks along the side and the shampoo in a large black bottle smelled of musk. When I was done I didn't see any towels other than a damp one already on the rack so I used a hand towel by the sink to dry myself and took a few laps around the apartment to allow the fresh air to complete the process. I put my clothes back on, poured myself a glass of orange juice from the refrigerator, and put on a different record. I didn't think it was the one that would have the song but it looked of the right vintage and was by an artist I hadn't heard of so it seemed worth trying. During my years in Washington and Oregon cloud cover had meant hooded sweatshirts, all-day lamps, afternoon naps, and early darkness. Looking out the window at the gray sky at that moment, though, knowing I would soon hear the song again, the clouds seemed a source of warmth and a buffer against time and circumstance. I thought again of Sei Shonagon, of spiraling footballs, and of my name in bold type on the cover of a book. When the record ended I felt neither disappointment nor concern. I put a different record on and grabbed a bagel from the refrigerator. Searching for a knife, I opened a drawer of random items: pencils, pens, a broken calculator, grocery coupons, a Swiss army knife, and a single key on a plastic ring, which I pocketed. When eventually I found a knife and toasted the bagel, the scent seemed sacred. I put the bagel on a plate and buttered it and sat in the chair by the window. A few minutes later Dennis and Oscar returned and nodded and toasted and buttered their own bagels. The three of us sat together for some quiet minutes, eating bagels and listening to an eighties album I knew would not contain the song but which, in its articulately-keyed urbanity, at least referenced the world in which the song existed. Dennis rose and disappeared down the apartment's hallway and Oscar put his plate in the sink and stood in the kitchen looking uncertainly about the place. I asked if there was a record he wanted to hear. He said he didn't know but if we were going to be there for a bit we probably needed "something chill."

"Why is it so hard for everyone to relax," he said. "We don't have anything we have to do or anywhere we have to go, but every little thing is apparently urgent. Everyone is always in a hurry for no reason."

"I'm not in a hurry," I said. "I'm just listening to records."

"Listening to someone else's records."

"First you were complaining about being in a hurry and now about listening to records. It doesn't make sense."

"I know Dennis has some Big Star albums. Have you seen them?"

I put one on. Dennis came back to the living room and he and Oscar sat on the couch and smoked. Oscar asked if I wanted any but I declined. I hoped if I sat quietly by the window I could stay indefinitely and I continue searching for the song. We were in the middle of the first side of the Big Star album, though, when it occurred to me Dennis might now be more disposed to chatting. "So what do you think about soft rock? I mean just in your opinion," I said.

"Again with the soft rock," he said.

"Do you have some seventies obscurities in your collection? Hidden gems?"

"I don't know. Is Gerry Rafferty obscure?"

"Gerry Rafferty is well-known."

"I have Al Stewart but Al Stewart doesn't qualify as obscure, either. Are you thinking about someone like Gary Wright?"

"'Dreamweaver' is famous. Maybe you have other one-hit wonders, though."

"Gary Wright isn't a one-hit wonder. He had two hits."

"What is the second?"

"'Love is Alive.'" Dennis began to sing about how his heart was on fire. When Oscar joined him for the next line—something about a wheel turning—I was momentarily stunned by how good they sounded. They didn't continue, though.

"I know that song," I said. "That's a good song."

"This is what I'm saying," Dennis said.

"But maybe you have actual one-hit wonders you play on occasion. I'm talking 10cc kind of stuff."

"10cc had three hits," he said. "'I'm Not in Love,' 'The Things We Do for Love,' and 'Dreadlock Holiday.' I won't sing them, though."

"But do you have a *section* for one-hit wonders? That's what I'm asking."

"You've got a real hard-on for one-hit wonders."

"It's just that the songs you've named aren't the one I heard."

"I'm sorry, but I don't think I can help you any more than I have. And you know, I've got something to do. I'm sure you guys have things to do, too."

He didn't strike me as the type of person who had many

obligations and I couldn't see what harm would come of me listening to records in his living room. I told him if he wanted, I could organize his records for him. I could do it alphabetically, or by genre, or alphabetically within genre, however he wanted.

"I already have them the way I like them, but thanks anyway," he said.

"Do you want me to clean them?" I said.

"Do I want you to what? No."

I pointed out that his shelves were a bit wobbly and I could brace them or tighten the hardware. He walked into the kitchen without answering.

"What is wrong with you?" Oscar said.

"Nothing is wrong with me. What's wrong with *you*?" I said.

Dennis returned and placed a bowl of potato chips in the middle of the coffee table and asked if I wanted a beer. I declined. We ate the chips and listened to Big Star. I asked Dennis if the thing he had to do was for work or for pleasure. "It really doesn't matter," he said. "I'm glad you like my records, but I wasn't looking to have a stranger hanging out in my apartment today. I've set this afternoon aside for something and I can't do it with you here. Do you understand that?"

"Sure, yes, I do," I said.

Oscar and I left. When we went our separate ways on the street he did little more than nod, and I walked back to my neighborhood alone. Refused access to the song yet again, I worried my attempts were pointless. Unless I did something soon, I would never become the person I wanted to be.

IV

I resumed my routine of YouTube, Sei Shonagon, and weed. Weeks passed. I stayed up late watching reality television reruns on obscure channels and then slept late and did little during the day. The song still existed and I knew it existed but its melody disappeared from my memory, leaving a void in the exact shape of the melody. The void was not an absence but a presence, like an empty billboard or a dead man's closet, and I lived with the billboard and the closet until I settled into the back of the line at a burrito cart one day and realized one of the three men in front of me was Dennis. When I said hello and asked what he was up to he said he and his friends were taking a lunch break from helping another friend move. I asked if they needed another hand.

"This isn't something you want to get involved in," he said. "This one's a bitch. It's going to take all day, if not longer."

"I'm not busy," I said.

"There are stairs and corners and my friend's uptight about everything. His parents are also there making things weird. You don't want any part of it."

"Fair enough. I hope it goes well," I said.

"Enjoy your burrito," he said.

When I got my burrito I walked back to my apartment and searched my belongings for the key I'd found in Dennis's junk drawer. I couldn't remember what I'd done with it. It was likely in the pockets of the pants I'd worn that day. But what pair had I worn? I alternated between jeans with a gray Dickies hoodie and chinos with a navy Carhartt hoodie. I was wearing the jeans and gray hoodie at the moment but the pockets did not hold the key. When I grabbed the chinos and navy hoodie from the floor of my closet and turned out their pockets, though, I found only grocery store receipts and granola bar crumbs. I checked counters and drawers and jars and shelves and was on the verge of tearing the cushions from my couch when I remembered I sometimes wore a pair of black jeans and a black and red plaid flannel shirt for social occasions, and I may have considered hanging out with Oscar a social occasion. I found the jeans and shirt at the bottom of the pile of clothes on the floor of my closet. In the change pocket of the jeans: the key! I shifted from despair to pride in having systems that worked and reminded myself that self-doubt was a bad habit, I was perfectly fine, and things were going in the right direction. These thoughts may have been an overcorrection but exulting in small victories at least has the benefit of supporting a positive mental attitude. I walked to Dennis's building, waited until a woman exited the ground level door, and timed my approach so that after she opened and passed through the security gate I slipped through in stride. When I climbed the stairs to the third floor and found Dennis's apartment, the door was locked. I tried the key, it turned, and I pushed the door open in a state of beatific gratitude.

The apartment was sunlit and peaceful. I turned on the stereo and played a record until I knew it wasn't the right one and then played a different one. If what Dennis had told me about his friend's move was true, I would have time to listen to a number of albums. There was a beer in the refrigerator and I drank it while eating my burrito. I would bring Dennis a six-pack the next time I visited, I told myself. After dismissing the album I was listening to and moving on to another, I opened the window that overlooked the street. Autumn sunlight slanted through the trees. The sky was thin and white and the breeze caused scattered leaves to let go their branches and flutter to the ground. Was soft rock vernal or autumnal? It is widely considered vernal but I decided at its core it was autumnal. I'd begun developing my argument on this point when my thoughts were interrupted by a knock on the door. "Hey! Stu!" a man called out. I sat still. It was an old building and the apartments were far from soundproof. Whoever was knocking could hear the music I was playing. He knocked again, harder. "Stu!" he shouted. "We need to talk!" Had I locked the door behind me when I came in? I couldn't remember. I discovered the answer a moment later, though, when the man pounded on the door and it shook in its frame. "Stu!" he yelled, trying and failing to open the door. His footsteps thundered down the hall and down the stairwell and I remained motionless for several minutes. When I was sure he was gone I tried some other records but not much later there was another knock at the door. I stayed as still as before as another male voice called through the door for Stu. This voice sounded confused rather than angry but also disappeared after a few minutes. The visitors made me nervous so I turned off the stereo, put the records away, and left by the stairway at the opposite end of the building. Did people have a mistaken apartment number or did Dennis go by different names? Was this door-pounding a common event? If so, how did the neighbors tolerate it? It was unfortunate, but I now had to question whether Dennis was in fact a person I could trust.

I called Oscar and told him I was in the mood for something adventurous. He said it was a bad idea. When I stopped by his place, though, he didn't refuse my money, and afterward I went straight back to Dennis's building. The light in his apartment was on and from the open window I heard faint music. I went to the gate and rang and when Dennis answered he asked what I could possibly want. I told him I was thinking about how I'd acted when I'd visited before and I had a small gift for him as an apology. The gate buzzed and I went up and found the door of his apartment open and Dennis inside on the couch. I pulled the Ziploc bag out of my pocket and handed it to him. "Holy shit," he said. "That's a serious apology. I was about to go to sleep, but I suppose it's still early." He went into the kitchen and I heard a cabinet open and the faucet run. When he returned he placed a pipe and a lighter on the coffee table. The pipe still had droplets of water in it and I realized he'd washed it. Was he always this clean or was it an act of courtesy? He loaded the pipe and said he assumed I wanted to smoke, too. "But first," he said, "did you get this from someone you trust?"

"I got it from Oscar," I said.

He laughed. "You got this from Oscar? Perfect. Have you smoked this before?"

"Not in a while."

"I can't believe I'm supposed to go to work in the morning."

He said he'd already called in sick a few times and was on the manager's bad side. When I asked where he worked he said he cooked at The Bean and Egg. Before The Bean and Egg he used to cook at Morning Becomes Egglectic, he said, and before that he cooked at a place called Hash and Dash but the owner there was even more unreliable than he was and the place went out of business. Before Hash and Dash he cooked at the Denny's on MLK. Before that he cooked at See You Bagel. He started at the counter there, he said, and that was the place he learned to cook, because a lady there was cool and showed him how to do everything. She really liked him, he said. The memory seemed to make him sad. I asked what he did before he cooked and he said just office work, boring stuff. He asked what I did and I told him I was writing a book on Heian-Era Japan and NFL Films. "You're writing two books?" he said.

"It's just one book," I said.

"And you're being paid?"

"No."

"So you have a trust fund or what's the deal?"

"My mom died and I got some money. That's all that happened."

"Okay. Sorry to hear that."

"Why did you laugh when I told you I got this from Oscar?"

"Because Oscar got this from me." He said Oscar had called

the previous day asking to buy more than a normal amount. It was obvious Oscar wanted to deal it, Dennis said. Dennis didn't like that but he needed money so he named a price he thought was way too high for Oscar to pay. Oscar showed up half an hour later with the money. "It solved a couple problems for me and I thought that was that," Dennis said. "I can't even imagine what he charged you. I'm sure this is my own shit, though, and I'm sure he ripped you off. Funny stuff. I'll be right back. And I wouldn't touch that if I were you. It's obvious you have no idea what you're doing."

He disappeared into the bathroom. While he was there I tipped a few more crystals into the pipe. When he came back he looked at it. The window that gave onto the street was closed and the room was silent. "Who even are you?" he said.

"Nobody," I said.

He inhaled deeply, as if considering a weighty proposition, and then exhaled all at once. "The problem with nobodies is they can be anybody. You never really know who a nobody is. Maybe that's their strategy or maybe it just happens naturally. If you claim you're one of these nobodies, maybe you can tell me whether it's a strategy or natural. I guess it could be a strategy that eventually became natural or something natural that turned into a strategy. I've thought of that, you know. I can think it through." He sat on the couch and grabbed his lighter and smoked some more and then flinched and dropped the pipe and put his hand to his mouth. "Fuck, I just burned myself. I never do that, I hate people who do that. It's sloppy and pathetic."

"I'll get some ice," I said.

"I don't need ice," he said.

"It sucks that what's left in there is going to be wasted."

I went to the kitchen and got a handful of ice from the freezer and wrapped it in a dishtowel and returned to the living room in time to see him setting the pipe on the table again. "I said I don't need ice!" he shouted. "Why did you get ice when I said I didn't need it?"

"I didn't hear you say anything about ice."

"You did so hear me say it. You were right here when I said it and you've been listening to every single thing I've said like you're recording it for history or something." He stood and walked to the kitchen and turned and came back to the living room. "You've been right here in the room with me the whole time, just watching me, and I don't know who you are or what the fuck you're up to, but it's time for you to go, friendo. It's way past time for you to go."

He was sweaty and red-faced and breathing hard. I told him I came over to apologize, that all of this was just a gift and I was sorry he was upset. "Are you sure you're okay being alone right now?" I said.

"You think I'm not okay? You're the one who's not okay.

Because I've been watching you, too, and you don't even know how to smoke. I don't think you've done this before at all. I think you just came here to trick me into showing you how to do it and now you're going to brag to people that you've smoked meth with me and that I'm your friend or something. You're going to act like you're a big deal."

"I have no idea who I would even say that to. I hardly even know anyone."

"You say you don't know anyone but the whole reason you're here is because you know someone. The whole reason you have the shit in the first place is because you know Oscar, so I know you know Oscar, which means that when you say you don't know anyone, you're lying. No one doesn't know anyone, by the way, that's just a stupid thing to say, an obvious lie. And now you're sitting here asking me if I'm okay being alone when being alone is actually the only thing I want. People are always acting like it's dangerous to be alone or sad to be alone or something's wrong with you if you want to be alone but let me tell you, the best times I have these days are when people finally leave me the fuck alone. I'm supposed to be rehearsing with my band, we're supposed to be recording, but no one ever leaves me alone so I can get any recording done. To book studio time I have to have money and in order to get money I have to go to work and stay focused, but instead, people are always bothering me."

"If you need money to book studio time I can lend you money," I said.

"So now you're trying to take over my band, too," he said. "You came over here to apologize, which is fake, and now you're trying to get me in debt to you. Get the fuck out of here before I beat the shit out of you."

"No problem," I said. "There's no problem here."

"There's definitely a fucking problem here," he said. "Get out. Now."

I left the apartment, crossed the street, and looked back. The light was still visible in the window. I could picture him pacing the length of the rooms and I could also picture him unconscious on the floor. I waited five minutes to see if he came to the window or turned out the light but nothing happened. I walked a few blocks, crossed the freeway, and pulled up the hood of my sweatshirt. The city still maintained pay phones at the light rail stations but the phone at the first station I came to was broken so I walked four blocks to the next station. The phone there worked and I dialed the emergency line, told the operator a person at Dennis's address and apartment number had overdosed, and hung up. I was able to walk all the way back to his building before anyone even showed up. So the authorities didn't feel the report of an overdose, a life or death circumstance, was worth responding to quickly! When a fire truck finally arrived I watched from down the block as two firemen walked through the gate and entered Dennis's building. An ambulance pulled up and two paramedics hopped out and also went in. A few minutes later one of them returned and unloaded a wheeled stretcher from the ambulance and pushed it into the building. He didn't seem to be in a hurry. A police car arrived and the firefighters came out of the building but the police officers never got out of their car. The system of who went in or out and when and why was impossible to discern. A group of twenty or thirty residents were standing together in the courtyard. A second, smaller group had gathered across the street and I joined them. Someone asked if anyone knew what was going on. "Probably domestic violence," a man said. "I haven't seen or heard anything at all," a woman said. "Domestic violence can be quiet. You wouldn't necessarily hear it," the man said. The woman said, "I just mean I haven't seen anyone who isn't a fireman or an EMT." There were various murmurs of agreement and the responses seemed to frustrate the man. "Anything is possible. None of us can really say," he said. He uttered the last in a tone that suggested he was chastising the woman, though the content of the statement could just as easily have been applied to his own claims. As others discussed the weather and attempted to count the number of responders, he retreated into a moody silence. I said nothing. After twenty minutes the paramedics came out with Dennis on the stretcher and loaded him into the ambulance. The vehicles left, the crowds dispersed, and I went home and slept soundly.

I came back the next morning, went through the gate via the hesitation-timing method, and used my key to enter the apartment, which was oddly clean for having hosted so many visitors the previous evening. The chair by the window had been moved crookedly next to the couch and a few magazines lay haphazardly open on the floor near a long sheet of half-crumpled paper that looked as if it may have lined the stretcher or served as equipment packaging. A carton of orange juice stood forgotten on the kitchen counter. It was half-full and room-temperature. What a waste, I thought. Dennis's pipe was nowhere to be seen.

I chose a record from the spot on the shelves where I'd left off, made myself a sandwich from some ham and a block of cheddar in the refrigerator, and began a new listening session. A few hours later there was a polite knock on the door. The situation had changed so this time I answered. An older man with glasses, curly gray hair, and tired eyes stood before me. He said he was Dennis's father and he was there to get some things for his son.

"What do you mean?" I said. "Where is Dennis?"

"Dennis is in the hospital. He took drugs last night and almost died."

"That's awful."

"I wasn't aware he had a roommate."

I explained I was a friend of Dennis's, we shared music collections, and Dennis had given me a key to listen to or borrow his records from time to time. I said Dennis had been doing a fair amount of drugs and spending time with untrustworthy people so I'd been keeping myself scarce. I'd been out with friends the previous evening and when I stopped by that morning the door had been unlocked, which I'd found odd.

"Somebody called the ambulance, which I'm glad of," Dennis's father said. "I'm less impressed the person didn't stay, but I suppose they were scared. Dennis is going to be gone for a while. He'll be going from the hospital straight to rehab. I hope this is a wake-up call for him, and for his friends."

"I don't know about his friends," I said. "But I haven't particularly liked the ones I've met."

"Be that as it may," he said.

I offered to watch the apartment in the short term and Dennis's father said that seemed fine. It was clear he didn't care who I was or whether I could be trusted, he just wanted to get his son's things. After he walked out the door with a white kitchen trash bag full of Dennis's clothes, I was alone and in possession of the apartment and the record collection.

V

I had a formidable task before me that I approached with discipline but also with moderation. More than a thousand albums filled the shelves along the apartment's living room wall. I could rule out albums from the nineties or later but that still left hundreds from the seventies and eighties. I moved some books and papers from my apartment to Dennis's apartment and walked there every morning to watch YouTube videos and write while listening to records. I assumed the people in the neighboring apartments would ask where Dennis had gone but only the immediate neighbors said anything. One of them, a young woman who said her name was Ashley, knocked on the door one afternoon to apologize for having had a party that ran late the previous evening. Her kitchen was on the other side of the wall from Dennis's kitchen. Ashley said now that she'd graduated college she and her boyfriend were going to move to San Francisco and she would be getting into fashion design. "Melody just started law school and is going to stay in the apartment, but I guess after this month I won't be seeing you anymore," she said. "It's been nice being neighbors, though." I hadn't met Melody so I wasn't sure what to do other than to say yes, it had been nice. Ashley laughed and said, "But as long as I'm still here I was wondering if you had any weed at the moment. Not much, maybe just the same as last time." There had been no last time and I realized Ashley thought I was Dennis. This was incomprehensible—Dennis and I looked nothing alike—but it seemed easiest to let it pass. I told Ashley I didn't have much but could give her enough for the evening. She waited while I retrieved the weed and when I returned to the door she handed me twenty dollars. "Thank you, Dennis. You're always prepared," she said. I told her she was welcome, wished her a nice evening, and she left none the wiser. I never met the roommate Melody but assumed hers was one of the muffled voices I heard through the kitchen wall over succeeding days. Dennis's stereo and speakers were on the far side of the apartment but if I turned the volume up too far Ashley would knock on the door and ask if I could turn it down. This seemed reasonable and for the most part I played music at an appropriate volume and Ashley and her roommate didn't bother me. It was unclear when Ashley was moving to San Francisco or if what she had said to me was an intention rather than a fact. I did not again speak to her directly. I'm not particularly chatty with neighbors in apartment buildings—I have never understood what is friendly and what is an overstep—but twice during my first week in Dennis's apartment I bought canned cookie dough and baked cookies in the evening as a way of signaling I meant no harm.

I established a productive routine: I smoked, worked on my book, and listened to Dennis's records. I understand this sounds inefficient as a means of discovering the song or maybe just as if I'd lost my sense of urgency but nothing could be further from the truth. It is just that detailing every aspect of my process would be tedious. Suffice to say I had a notebook in which I listed the albums I'd listened to, the date I'd listened to them, and notes on their sound. After only two weeks, however, I flipped the turntable power on one afternoon and nothing happened. I am not mechanically inclined and after checking the connections and plugs and finding nothing amiss my project was stalled. I did not own a turntable myself and didn't know anyone I could borrow one from—I would have to repair Dennis's. I knew of a stereo store on Hawthorne Avenue but it had bars on the windows and the entrance was in the back and it didn't have a website so I ruled it out. There was another on Morrison but when I looked it up it turned out they had recently gone out of business. In desperation I began repeatedly turning the player's power switch on and off and at some point it started. I was overjoyed and listened to one album side but when I switched the player off in order to flip the record I couldn't get it to turn back on. I sat there staring at the wall of records, trying and failing to recall the melody of the song I was looking for. Each time I tried, a different song's melody entered my mind. I worried the song, the key to my health and success in life, would fade permanently from my memory. There is an episode of *The Twilight Zone* in which a nearsighted reader in postapocalyptic solitude is overjoyed to find himself surrounded by books but immediately breaks his glasses. I was living a variation of that story and it was a nightmare.

I put the turntable in a box I found in Dennis's closet and loaded the box into my car. I told myself this was a minor setback, nothing serious. Plenty of young people in Portland were buying record players, so there would have to be repair shops. I drove to the store on Hawthorne and willed myself to ignore the barred windows and to go around back and enter. The space was smaller than I expected and crowded with tables and glass cases and strange devices. A middle-aged salesman asked if I needed help and I explained I had a record player in need of repair. "I'm sorry, we sell players but we don't service them," he said.

"I'm pretty sure it's just the power switch," I said. "I don't think it's complicated."

"The whole thing is really just a switch, a motor, and a belt," he said.

"Unfortunately, all three of those things are beyond me. Is there a place you recommend?"

"There's a young guy who works here said he takes his downtown. It's on Washington, I think. Big sign."

"How big?"

"I mean, it's not a billboard. It's a sign."

"So somewhere between a small street sign and a big billboard. Thanks a lot, chief."

"Sorry I'm not the yellow pages," he said.

"The what?"

"The yellow pages. The thing you could use to look this up on your own."

"The yellow pages? What year do you think this is?"

"Thanks for stopping in. The door is right there."

I asked if he was a time traveler from the nineteen eighties who was trying to save the future by working in a little store with bars on the windows without realizing no one used the yellow pages anymore. I wondered aloud what kind of problem in the past would require him to speak in riddles about signs that were not small but not billboards. His mission seemed tricky.

"Tremendous," he said. "Fantastic material. Thanks so much. Have a great day."

"Don't worry, I will. I'm off to look for a big sign."

I drove directly downtown and found the store on Washington without much difficulty. It had what I felt was a medium-size sign that said Continuous Groove. The store was long and narrow and when an employee saw the turntable box in my arms he directed me up a set of metal stairs at the side of the store. The stairs led to a loft level at the back of which a balding man sat looking at an audio receiver in pieces before him on a desk. I had never been in a stereo store proper and considered myself neither rich nor an audiophile so this all seemed very exotic. The man looked at me over the rims of his glasses and suggested I set my box on a table to the side. He asked what the problem was and I told him it was just that the power switch didn't work.

"In which direction," he said.

"I don't understand," I said.

"The power on or the power off?"

"It won't turn on."

"That is always the way," he said. "I've never seen the opposite."

"But do you think it's worth fixing?"

"If it's worth playing, it's worth fixing."

I considered the statement. "I don't think I know what that means."

"I'll take a look at it," he said. "Not now, though. I'll give you a call."

He did not smile or end his statement in any service-friendly way and after filling out a brief form I had to decide on my own that our interaction was concluded and I should leave.

When I returned to Dennis's apartment I looked at the empty spot where the turntable had been and realized I had lost all possibility of making headway in my search. Why had I not just bought my own player? Why was I being so stupid? I liked to think of myself as self-sufficient but these reflections were troubling. Taking a broken turntable to be repaired was responsible, I thought, but there was also something odd about it. What I lacked, I thought, was the quality of being what people called *self-actualized*. The difference between *self-sufficient* and *self-actualized* seemed slight but important and I needed to focus not on the former but on the latter.

I went to Music Millennium and bought a mid-tier turntable and hooked it up to Dennis's stereo. I wrote and watched YouTubes and listened to records. I didn't discover the song and many of the records I played were in styles that made it immediately clear they wouldn't have the song but I played these records in full, regardless. I had a project: my book. The leaves on the neighborhood trees turned rust and gold. I had a project: the song. The evenings grew crisp and settled. Was I a complete person? No. I hadn't completed my book. I didn't know the song. But was I on the path? Yes, I was.

Someone from the stereo store called to tell me my turntable was ready. I went to the store and climbed the stairs and discovered that in the intervening days the loft had been reorganized to mimic a long, narrow apartment. The effort was minimal and unrealistic and seemed inspired by the kinds of apartments lived in by young adult characters on television shows or by a teenager's dream of what a city "artist's loft" might look like. I found the set-up slick and bourgeois in a way the rest of the store was not and wondered if it betrayed a change in management. I walked through the model living room and the false kitchen to the back of the loft where the same man I had met before stepped from behind his desk. He was taller than I remembered, with an immaculately clipped fringe of hair that ringed the sides and back of his otherwise bald scalp. He wore a bright white dress shirt and gray flannel slacks and looked to be in his sixties, though I place all bald men in their sixties. His expression was as neutral as the décor, as if the loft were a tank and he its fish. I was surprised, however, to notice he wore bright white tennis shoes. They did not seem to fit his outfit or aesthetic and I wondered if maybe this was how a stereo salesman from the nineteen eighties naturally aged. When I told him I was there to pick up the turntable he said, "Ah. Then you are a person I have some questions for. It's an interesting machine. I've hooked it up in the living room."

I followed him to a metal shelving unit against the brick wall in the ersatz apartment. The turntable was one of three in the shelving unit's grid, each player set carefully in the center of its particular shelf. The shelves also held five different receivers and too many sets of speakers to count. A green velvet couch and two matching armchairs faced the shelves and a black leather motorcycle jacket hung on a peg on the brick wall. I couldn't tell if the jacket belonged to the man I was speaking to or if it was part of the decor.

"I won't pretend to know how many places in town are doing brisk business in used turntables, but I'm so busy with them these days the store is thinking of hiring a second technician," he said. "My name is Baker, I'm in charge of repairs here."

"Were you able to fix mine?" I asked.

"It wasn't complicated," he said. "You were right, the problem was the switch. But there's something I wanted to ask about. You see, I record the serial number of every machine I work on. I've been in business a long time and so of course I have a lot of serial numbers. When I entered your machine's number into the computer, it turned out I've fixed this machine before."

"I'm borrowing it from a friend," I said. "He must have brought it here for service."

"That's possible. Or maybe your friend bought the turntable from someone else and that someone else brought it here. A good turntable can pass through a number of owners. Didn't Jack London write books about dogs who have multiple owners?"

"I think the idea has been done a number of times."

"Has it been done about turntables?"

"Other objects."

"I see. Well, the thing that distinguishes turntables is the quality of the motor. The belts can be replaced. An arm can be replaced. Even the plate can be replaced if you really want to, though at that point you have to wonder if what you really need is a new turntable. Needles and cartridges are of course disposable. My point is just that if the motor is sound, it can run for decades."

"How long have you been in the stereo business?" I asked.

"Straight out of high school," he said. "Back then there were courses you could take in record player and sewing machine repair, refrigerator or television repair, things like that. I wasn't interested in refrigerators or televisions but I fixed sewing machines and record players at a general repair shop. Sewing machines are fascinating—they can get quite ornate. But record players were where it was at. When hi-fi came in with all the sixties rock and jazz, setting up stereo systems was a kick. I know this is an old-man thing to say, but audio quality has gone down. I'm speaking as a person who has listened closely to music through every kind of audio system from the nineteen fifties to now. It's a well-known fact in the industry that there have been no technological advances since the early eighties. You can vary bass and treble levels in speakers or headphones to make things sound different or distinct, and you can change the colors of the plastic or metal you put your product in, but audio systems themselves stopped improving long ago. Personally, I think the high point was the late seventies. Here, I'll show you something."

He plugged my record player into a power strip and connected it to an old receiver whose analog AM/FM continuum glowed blue-green. A high shelf held a couple dozen albums. He pulled one down, plucked the disc from the sleeve, and placed it on the player.

"Let me demonstrate that your turntable is repaired by playing something from that era," he said, lowering the needle. "If we consider the idea of fidelity—"

"Is that piano here in the loft?" I said.

"Just wait," he said.

A drummer and a bass player joined the piano. "Who is this?" I said.

"Ford Halliday. He only had a couple albums with hits on them. Seventy-six and seventy-eight, I believe."

"Who is playing the saxophone?"

He looked at the sleeve. "It doesn't say. The albums with hits were maybe seventy-eight and eighty."

"Is Halliday playing the electric guitar or the acoustic?"

"I assume it's overdubbed, so probably both. They're his songs and mostly his playing."

Each section of the song we listened to unfolded at such a confident, unhurried pace that I could only assume Halliday had been classically trained. I don't mean the song sounded like classical music. Musicians who try to blend rock and classical music fail. They adopt surface qualities of classical music, like numbered movements or variations on a theme, but for no reason and to little effect. What I was listening to was a carefully-constructed song that would have been equally at home on the playlists of a classic rock station or an easy listening station. It would work in a grocery store or a bank but also during a day at the beach or on a late-night drive. A cello entered at the bridge, joined by violins. Different instruments featured in compact solos that together conveyed a sense of orchestral abundance. I am not a person who knows much about drums but the steady beat and transitional fills stunned me. The rhythm was precise and functional and it was clear the drummer knew his role. Halliday's vocal was simple and competent but what struck me was how little he had to do as a singer. The song's structure carried everything along. All that was required of him was to be present. I would ascribe the effectiveness of his singing to the genius of the song rather than to Halliday himself, but Halliday was of course also the person who had written the song. The man had built the vessel now carrying him, had created the event he needed now only to attend. As the song continued I felt it was expanding the dimensions of the building itself. (When I later listened to the song in other rooms, though, I experienced it as intimate rather than epic, and when it played while I was reading or writing it could slip past without my even noticing.) The electric guitar solo was operatic. Its tones returned me instantly to childhood but the solo rose so dramatically that it also suggested the composition and recording—the entire context of the song's production—had occurred in a mist I might soar through like a hawk above forest treetops. While Baker adjusted the sliders of a small equalizer I forgot the purpose of my visit. He had us flying. The sonic illusion, which would have been arresting in any room, was enhanced by the elevation of the loft and our nearness to the building's wooden ceiling beams. "I suppose that demonstrates the unit is working," he said. He lifted the needle and unplugged the player from the receiver. "Thank you for your business. It was lovely to see this machine again. I can take payment over at the desk."

"It won't sound the same at home," I said. "I'll have to remember all of the qualities of your system here."

"Visit whenever you like," he said.

I paid, carried the turntable to my car, and drove straight across the river to Music Millennium. It took me no more than five minutes to find and buy a new 180-gram pressing of the Halliday album. There was a satisfying heft to it and I placed it carefully on the passenger seat. Even in silence it emanated a sublime benevolence. Dennis had better speakers but his apartment was farther away. There was also the issue of Ashley and her roommate and the volume, as well as the fact that the turntable I'd just had repaired, now in a box in the back seat, was easily the superior player. I decided it would be best to go straight to my own apartment.

I tried to head there via a commercial street, but an accident near the park had traffic backed up. I chose a second route but was waylaid when orange-vested workers stopped traffic while a truck loaded with sheetrock crept slowly onto the lot of a building under construction. I was boxed in. Try to make art and the world will stop you. Try merely to appreciate it and even then, here comes traffic. When the workers let us go I turned onto a residential street. Crows scattered before my roaring approach and I shouted after them. When I finally made it to my building, carried everything inside, and realized I had no audio cables to connect the player to the receiver, I unleashed a stream of violent language, took everything back to the car, and snaked through multiple residential blocks until I could cross into northeast Portland and make my way to Dennis's apartment. I won't bore you with the details of connecting the components again other than to mention that even though I was the one who had unhooked Dennis's turntable, all of the plugging and unplugging had taken a toll and when the system at first produced no sound I nearly threw everything out the window. I realized I had transposed two cables, though, and when I fixed the error and dropped the needle on the Halliday song, the magic began. Here was the casual confidence, the implied orchestra, the mist and the hawk. If I listened to this song at least once a day, I told myself, I would be happy.

So this is how, drifting and lost, I recovered my sense of self. In pursuit of one song, I found another—with the assistance of a broken turntable and a private record collection. I moved into Dennis's apartment, started my days with coffee and a bagel, put on an album, and worked on my book. After a few hours of writing I walked to the food carts for a burrito or a rice bowl. I kept a notebook in which I recorded the names of the albums I listened to and made sure to listen to something new every day. At the end of each day I played the Halliday track to reset my levels, my expectations, and my mood. The mist! The hawk! In the evenings I smoked, walked the city, and returned home to watch a movie or a show. I heard nothing from Dennis or his family, had yet to identify the song, and enjoyed what were probably the best weeks of my life. I believed that if and when Dennis returned he would see I had taken exceptional care of his apartment and things and he might reward me with the name of the song. If he couldn't identify or didn't know the song, I would understand, because I had achieved it! In those few weeks of my life I was centered, focused, and easygoing. Everything that came after—with Dennis, his father, Oscar, the police—was of course a mess and not worth going into here. Eventually technology solved the mystery of the song for me. Because it's not a matter of importance to me anymore I forget the name, but it's the one by Starbuck.

Propeller Books Titles

Louise Akers, *Elizabeth/The Story of Drone*
Wendy Bourgeois, *The Devil Says Maybe I Like It*
Dan DeWeese, *Gielgud*
    Disorder
Miriam Gershow, *Survival Tips (forthcoming)*
Kirsten Ihns, *sundaey*
Elizabeth Lopeman, *Trans Europe Express*
Patrick McGinty, *Test Drive*
Mary Rechner, *Marrying Friends (forthcoming)*
    Nine Simple Patterns for Complicated Women
Matthew Robinson, *The Horse Latitudes*
Evan P. Schneider, *A Simple Machine, Like the Lever*
Abraham Smith, *Dear Weirdo*
Tony Wolk, *The Parable of You*

Northwest Collection Editions

Sheila Evans, *The Northport Stories*
    (introduction by Dan DeWeese)
Alan Hart, *The Undaunted*
    (foreword by Carter Sickels)
Mary Rechner, *Nine Simple Patterns for Complicated Women*
    (foreword by Miriam Gershow)
Evan P. Schneider, *A Simple Machine, Like the Lever*
    (foreword by Justin Hocking)

Printed in the USA
CPSIA information can be obtained
at www.ICGtesting.com
LVHW041618290923
759456LV00004B/129